# Twisted Tales of Somerset and North Devon

by Jo Harthan

**Twisted Tales of Somerset and North Devon**.

Illustrations, Artwork and Photographs: Joan C. Harthan





ISBN-13: 978-1542911375

ISBN-10: 1542911370

**FRONT COVER -** Digital collage of the Minehead Obby Oss

# Contents

***The magnificent sculpture in Minehead, marking the start of the South West Coast Path.***

## FOREWORD

This collection of short stories was inspired and created on the first section of the South West Coast Path of England. It was 2008 when I took the first intrepid steps from Minehead, in Somerset, heading for Poole in Dorset, six hundred and thirty miles away. Grabbing long weekends here and there, I hiked my way southward, up and down the Somerset combes and onto the plunging valleys and rocky peaks of the North Devon coastline, eventually crossing over into Cornwall at an overgrown gulley a little north of Morwenstow.

The whole of the South West Coast Path is stunning, with its dramatic landscapes and wild seas, but this section has a beauty all of its own. It is a steep rugged coastline with unforgiving cliffs separated by gouged out combes where the path falls precipitously down to the shoreline and then climbs steeply back up onto the cliffs. Generally only serious walkers will attempt this challenging terrain and so this section of the path tends to be quieter than some of the Cornish and South Devon sections. It also means that accommodation is more affordable - an added bonus when you've got over six hundred miles ahead of you. I mostly used friendly B & Bs on this stretch, enjoying a first-rate English breakfast at the start of each day's trek - you need plenty of calories on a walk like this!

The stories in this collection are a mixture of fact and fiction. The places are factual and provide the backdrop to these gruesome tales. The people and situations, on the other hand, are fictitious, though now they have been given life in these stories it is unlikely that they will rest easy in their literary confinement. Reality, after all, is what is inside our own heads.

Let us begin in Minehead, where we will join Megan as she follows the hobby horse parade around the town on May Day Eve. As Megan's evening progresses, we will be reminded how important it is to be very careful what you wish for, especially where dark horses are concerned.

From there we will travel southward to Culbone and the beautiful little church that nestles in the woods. We may stop here longer than we intend for there has been some sort of slippage and the Fairies are up to mischief again.

Our next stop will be Lynmouth and Lynton, where we hear about a most peculiar accident on the funicular railway that ferries tourists up and down the cliff between the two historic towns. If we survive the cataclysmic event that follows, we will trek on to Glenthorne, where wild boar roam the woods and a beautiful woman ensnares lonely travellers. If you do ever venture down that way and happen upon her, be sure not to do as she asks, otherwise you may be one of those unfortunates who are eternally damned for your indiscretion.

Our next stop will be on the sprawling cairn at the top of Great Hangman where, down below on Rawn's Rocks, we will be faced with the full horror of our own death and the fate of all humankind.

Assuming we have a stay of execution, we will travel down to Appledore, a sleepy, picturesque fishing village just north east of Westward Ho! Here we find Liz, let down by her friend yet again, venturing out to stave off her dark mood. Little does she know that a fate far worse than melancholia is waiting for her out on the lane.

Our journey ends at Embury Beacon where Ella and her father are having a picnic, making up for all the years they have been apart. But all is not as it seems and poor Ella gets a lot less than she bargained for.

So, sit back and enjoy this collection of twisted tales for, according to a retired Professor living in Lynmouth, it may be the last book you ever read!

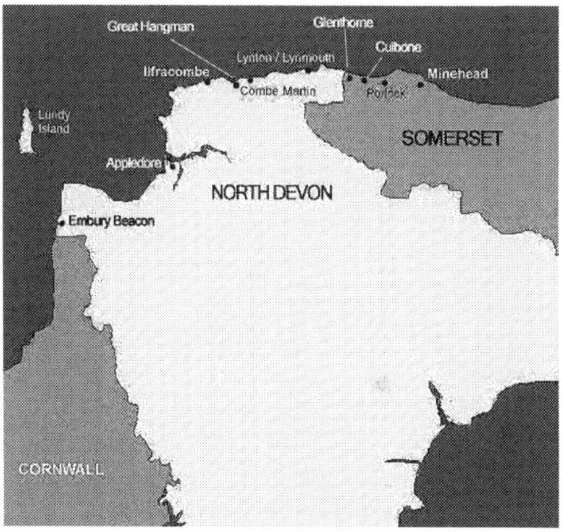


***Map of Somerset and North Devon***
***showing the settings for these Twisted Tales.***

# The Hobby Horse Tradition

***Photograph showing the Minehead Hobby Horse in bygone days. Reproduced here by kind permission of http://mineheadonline.co.uk.***

The hobby horse, which bears little resemblance to the real animal, traditionally welcomes the Spring, the season of fertility.

In England, this tradition goes back to the island's early pagan roots, though its origin is lost in time. The first recorded mention of these strange horses is in the mid-16th century when they were associated with Morris dancing, another fertility tradition.

In modern times, though the pagan roots of the hobby horse are either forgotten or ignored they do dance through towns during May festivals, the time of the pagan Beltane celebrations. At one time towns all over England had hobby horses, but most were discontinued during the last century and not many are left today. Of those that remain, the best known are at Padstow and Minehead.

As regards the origin of these odd creatures, we can only speculate. One theory is that the more familiar hobby horse, in the form of a simple pole with a horse's head on top, is a forerunner to the more elaborate forms seen in the opening illustration. Yet even these simple toys are believed to have an ancient provenance. The idea that they were fashioned in the style of witches' broomsticks is not new. Broomsticks were reputedly used during fertility orgies, when the wooden pole of the broom would be smeared in an hallucinatory substance, easily absorbed through the mucus membranes of the naked genitalia. Our modern hobby horse parades may not have such extreme rituals but they have always been rowdy occasions, with dancing and drinking, as is fitting for a pagan fertility celebration.

Perhaps because of the assumed pagan roots, the hobby horse tradition has a somewhat sinister nature. This was captured very well in the cult film The Wicker Man, where a hobby horse took part in the pagan parade prior to the burning of the naive, Christian policeman played by Edward Woodward.

This provides a very fitting prelude to my first story; The Minehead Obby Oss.

# The Minehead Obby Oss

It was May Day Eve. Show Night, according to the information Megan had got from the town library. She had popped in yesterday hoping to find some local event to take her mind off the break-up with Charley, and it looked like she had found just the ticket. Peering out of the window of her rented cottage down at the harbour, she could see the revellers assembled outside 'The Old Ship Aground' at the quay, waiting for the annual Obby Oss parade to begin.

The move to Minehead was to have been a new start for her and Charley, neutral ground where they could mend the rift that had grown between them. As it turned out, he had never moved in, telling her at the eleventh hour that he thought they should split, no discussion, no reason.

They had already paid the bond and so she moved in anyway, with a part of her hoping he would come to his senses and join her. Hope doesn't cost anything after all.

"Come on," she told herself, "no good moping about."

Grabbing a light cotton jacket that was hung by the door, she stepped outside. It was a warm spring evening and a gentle breeze was carrying the offbeat sounds of drums and accordions along the harbour. The musicians, looking flushed with beer and good cheer, were singing bawdily, not seeming to care if they were in tune or not. The crowd was roaring with excitement and anticipation. This was just what she needed, an evening of frivolity and fun.

As she approached along Quay West, she could see the horse adorned with fluttering strips of bright cloth and could hear the musicians encouraging the crowd to sing along,

'. . . *Sailor's Horse is in our blood. We always do it right. Down on the quay, watching the Minehead swell . . .*'

And then down the horse came toward her in full view, cavorting along the road like a ship on a swollen sea. Nothing more than a wooden frame carried on the shoulders of someone hidden inside, and yet it seemed to have a life of its own. Covered in ribbons and scraps of brightly coloured rags, it had a cloth hanging down to the ground, gaily painted with multicoloured roundels. A long rope tail swished this way and that, purposely hitting the onlookers, making the children squeal. Its gaping mouth leered at the world, exposing two rows of razor sharp teeth.

Stopping briefly, it faced up to a clutter of teenage boys on the pavement, standing with hands in pockets, looking tough and unimpressed. The white face, made of tin, with its shiny red nose and painted scarlet cheeks, jibed at them but they stared it down with their sulky gaze until it moved on. The next moment it was right in front of Megan. She could see the sparkling eyes of the man inside.

"Come, follow me," he said.

And follow she did, along with many of the town's people and a host of tourists. Along the quay they went with the horse swaying, bouncing, twizzing and twirling, followed by men banging thin sticks on taut drums, yelling and shouting, and the accordionists playing a repetitive, hypnotic melody.

Every so often, the horse bowed to onlookers, dropping the front down and sweeping along the ground. All the while, the Sailor's Colt cavorted around, joined now by the Town Horse adorned with jingling bells. Not as colourful as the Sailor's Horse, but more energetic by far. Prancing to and fro, pirouetting, leaping into the air, doing obeisance to onlookers, especially the affluent looking ones - no doubt hoping for a large donation. They were soon joined by another, The Sailorette, all dressed in pink, stepping lightly across the paving. Up Clanville Road they went, hardly slowing their pace despite the climb, up onto Holloway and into Church Street.

And then it happened. Just as they reached Church Steps, a black hobby horse charged round the corner from Vicarage Road and into the crowd. Dark ribbons fluttered across its back and a black skirt hung from the frame, splashed with muted roundels that looked like eyes poking up through a peat bog. The name Black Devil was embroidered in bold stitching across its body. Young girls cried as it rushed towards them, cornering them, pushing them to the ground, in danger of being trampled. The men ran to their aid only to be knocked off their feet by the heavy frame of the horse slamming into them. An angry voice from inside the frame was chanting,

"Oh one, oh two, oh three . . ."

Right on up to ten; its booted feet striking its victims with each number called. Onlookers scuttled out of the way. Those that escaped the kicks were in danger of being slashed by the barbed tail that was swinging around viciously. The women screamed. Chaos ensued.

Megan looked on in horror. There was a shadowy mist circling around the dark horse, like sweat in a sauna, clinging and rolling. From the mist came dark strands, sprouting out in all directions, spreading like fungus - a parasite looking for a new host.

Then time seemed to stand still for Megan. The horse stopped its carnage and slowly turned its head in her direction. A black cat, with a squawking magpie in its mouth, slunk across the road in front of her and disappeared under a garden gate as the gruesome horse advanced, its neck swaying hypnotically to and fro. The next moment, it was before her. Black eye sockets, outlined with red, filled with darkness. Megan felt the pull. It was like falling into a black hole from which no light can ever escape. Panic rose up in the pit of her stomach. She had to get away.

With a tremendous effort she broke free, pushing through the screaming crowd, and set off running back down towards the quay, praying she would get home before the last rays of the sun disappeared.

She had not gone far when she stopped in her tracks. Someone or something was following her. She could feel it. Plucking up the last of her courage, she turned round. Fungal-like tendrils were flowing along behind her, swirling and curling into a semi-human form that crouched and crept closer, embracing, holding on tight. It felt cold and slimy like a body too long in the grave. Megan had seen things like this before but had always explained them away; shadows, movement, light playing tricks, things not quite there. But in that moment there was no doubt. She could see it as plainly as if she were looking at the dark side of the moon in full sunlight. There was no explaining this away. This was real and she didn't know how to get rid of it. She needed help, someone who knew what they were doing.

She remembered Mr. Khalifa; a shamanic practitioner up on Whitecross Lane. She had seen his advertisements in the local paper and had nearly rung him more than once in the hope that he might give her news about Charley. His adverts said he was available for healing and divining the future. She would go and see him. She would go now, right away. He would know what to do.

Not wishing to confront the Black Devil again, she went via the town and up onto The Parks, taking the steep path that leads from the end of Periton Lane, bringing her out almost adjacent to Mr. Khalifa's house. Unlike its neighbours, which had well-kept gardens and fancy names, the windows of number thirteen were dirty and the render was old and discoloured. Megan had passed the house many times, intrigued and yet a little wary. It was the only house on the lane with its view over the town mostly hidden from view by an unkempt hedgerow. Apart from the house, the only thing that could be seen from the road was a tall, wire matchstick man standing near the gate, offering a plate of crumbs to the wild birds.

This evening, curiously, the garden gate was open, normally it was closed. She walked through and followed the winding, overgrown path to the house. Strange occult-looking objects were half hidden in the grass, interspersed with sculptures of animals carefully placed so as to give the impression of watchfulness; a wolf whose eyes seemed to follow her, a wild cat poised to pounce, a goat with head bowed ready to butt intruders. Her eyes were drawn to three statuesque ravens perched in a holly bush. They seemed to be moving; perhaps it was just the breeze, or maybe her eyes were playing tricks in the gathering gloom. At their side was a dream-catcher, lit up at the centre with a strange blue light and surrounded by twinkling fairy lights strung haphazardly within the branches. Making her way to the front door, she had to pass by them and she shivered at the feeling of impending doom they imparted. She wondered whether she should just go home.

The front door had been painted in a glossy red paint that was peeling away to reveal a dull shade of green underneath. Standing at the side was a statue of Christopher Lee depicted as Saruman from Tolkein's Lord of the Rings, easily recognisable since Peter Jackson's immortalisation of the tales for the big screen. Why Saruman, she wondered? Why not Gandalph?

She knocked on the door and waited, glancing behind every so often. It was still there. The thing. The shadow, with its tendrils of infection. She knocked again. Still no answer.

Peering in through the window, she saw the room was in darkness. There was no one home. She turned to go.

"That which follows you is Old Mother Leakey," the voice, sounding distant and enclosed, was coming from the direction of a shed at the far side of the garden. She peered into the fading light but all she could see was a life-size statue of a grizzly bear standing on the path that ran to the back of the house, as if guarding the entrance to another world.

"Excuse me? I can't see you. Where are you?"

"Here my dear," a man said as he emerged from the shed, carefully locking it behind him. He was broad-shouldered and stocky like the bear, though not as tall. As he came closer, a security light exploded into the darkness, showering him with harsh, white light. Megan's eyes were drawn to a bright red neckerchief tied around his neck, a total mismatch to the loose fitting, lime green shirt. She thought how mean his mouth looked, with its thin lips and taut smile, but dismissed the thought immediately, wanting to savour the relief she felt, knowing she would not have to spend time convincing him of her plight.

"You can see her?" she asked.

"Yes I can see her, a troublesome ghost from the 17th century. She's come again in the devil's likeness, just as she promised she would."

"Why me? Why would she come to me?"

"You must have an intrusion. Something that's attracting her."

"You mean I'm possessed?"

"Not exactly. An intrusion is like a squatter who finds a vacant room in your house and moves in uninvited."

"Can you help?"

"Of course. Please, come inside."

The inside of the house was as strange as the garden, with all manner of exotic paraphernalia lying around. Drums and rattles placed on low tables, shrunken heads hung on walls. A strong smell of sage wafted through the air.

"Have you had any trauma lately?" Mr. Khalifa asked once they were seated.

Megan could feel the power he carried and knew it would be useless to lie.

"I split with my boyfriend a couple of months ago."

"And you want him back? You're pining for him?"

She found his directness embarrassing but she nodded anyway because his words, like an arrow shot by a trained archer, hit the target straight on.

"Sometimes when we love someone," he said, taking her hand, "they take a piece of our soul. If they leave without giving it back, it leaves a hole inside. Right here," he hit his chest in a dramatic gesture. "A spare room where anything can take up residence."

"So what's moved in? Can you see it?"

"Yes I can see it. It's a recent tenant, not settled in yet."

"It was the black hobby horse. It came right up to me. I felt it."

"You're very perceptive my dear."

"Can you get rid of it for me?"

"Yes I can do that."

"Can you do it now?"

Mr. Khalifa looked at his watch, looking thoughtful as if he had something else planned,

"It's rather late. But yes, we don't want you attracting anything else while you sleep."

"Once it's gone, could you make my boyfriend come back?" The words spewed out of her mouth without warning, leaving her feeling embarrassed and ridiculously hopeful.

He shook his head, "I could, but that's not ethical. And even if I did, he'd only leave again. I'll do an extraction; get rid of the intrusion. Then I'll retrieve the part of your soul that your boyfriend took. But none of this will get rid of old mother Leakey. Though with the intrusion gone she'll likely grow tired of following you and leave of her own accord."

*                    *                    *

Two hours later and Megan was heading back home down Whitecross Lane, escorted by Mr. Khalifa. Although his house was close to the town, it was high on the hill and the surrounding lanes were deserted during the hours of darkness.

"Not a lane for young women to walk down alone at night", he had said, "especially when being followed by old mother Leakey."

He had kindly prepared a herbal tea to help her sleep and had assured her that the intrusion was gone and that old mother Leakey would soon depart for more fertile ground. The rituals he had performed, although costly, had been relaxing and empowering, and she believed wholeheartedly that she was now free of the darkness that had attached itself to her. It was not until she got into bed that she began to doubt the efficacy of the treatment.

It started with a vague shadow in the corner of the room, slightly darker than all the other shadows. And then it moved, coming closer, and closer, until she could see the dark outline of the face; a face that she recognised.

"What are you doing here?" she gasped.

There was no answer but a hand was placed on the pillow.

"I've wanted so much for you to come back," she said, "I've missed you."

He pulled back the duvet and slid in beside her. His touch was warm and tender, just like it used to be. She yielded to the pressure of his hands, which held her firm. Was this a dream? Was she still sleeping? She turned her head to look at the clock on the bedside table. Its cheerful red glow said it was 3am. Everything looked just as it should. Warm breath washed over her face as he crawled on top of her. She felt him enter her. Rhythmic, pulsing, groaning. How she'd missed this, missed him. And yet, it did not feel like it used to feel. Something was not right. The moment she had that thought, he was gone, as if he had never been.

She had read about lucid dreams, about how they could seem more real than real life. Was that what just happened? With a trembling hand she switched on the bedside lamp. That was when she saw it, a small black shape lying on the pillow. It looked like a beetle and she let out a scream. But no, it wasn't a beetle. She picked it up and held it towards the light. It was a tiny black horse, no more than a centimetre long, its face painted in the style of the Black Devil hobby horse. Tied neatly around its neck was a small red neckerchief - exactly like the one Mr. Khalifa had been wearing.

*'The Minehead Obby Oss'*

Like clowns in a circus, these strange hobby horse creatures have always held a primal fascination. They provide a mask, a false identity, for the person inside who has unspoken permission to get up to all sorts of mischief. The Black Devil hobby horse in Minehead fired my imagination in the direction of my macabre story, purely and simply because anything with that name cannot fail but give the impression of dark deeds and evil intentions.

# Culled At Culbone

It was Good Friday, a propitious time for the living to meet with the dead.

I had left Porlock in the morning, with fourteen miles of the South West Coast Path lying ahead of me, including more than ten Somerset combes, each one as challenging as the steepest Lakeland peaks. I had been on the path less than an hour when, through a heavily pruned hedgerow, I spied a wild garden laid with concentric rings of spring daffodils. A path of mown grass spiralled down to the remains of an ancient oak in the centre, its trunk cleaved in two by the hand of decay. It was how I imagined a Fairy Ring would look, untidy, magical. All around were oak and holly with their rich, contrasting shades of green, brightened from below with yellow primroses and white dog rose, made sweeter by the call of blackbirds and wrens who filled the air with song.

As I breathed in the beauty before me, a small figure appeared near the centre as if from nowhere; its gossamer wings flittering in the breeze. A butterfly perhaps? No, too large and yet still so small. A golden glow shone around legs that danced in the sunlight. Recognition pulled aside the thin veil that separates the worlds. This was a nature spirit from the land of Fairie. I held my breath lest I should be spotted, but the figure turned, saw me, and then it was gone, taking with it the old world I had grown to love. That solitary, magical figure ushered in a new life, a new future, a future I neither chose nor wanted.

As if in a dream, I continued on my way, passing through the arched toll gate at the top of Worthy Combe, and found myself on an enclosed walkway. The path skirted a building that had the stone battlements of a medieval castle, yet woven with the thatched roof of a workman's cottage. It was a strange mixture that fed my dazed countenance. Passing under two stone arches that sheltered a thick carpet of dead leaves, the way became deep and hushed and dank. Stone walls stood either side, covered in thick green moss, with tendrils of ivy hanging down. I breathed in the strange scent of an elfish land that time had forgotten.

The path led me into Yearnor Wood where the yellow sun cascaded through silver branches in golden rivers of light. There I saw more fairy forms, twinkling as they swam upstream. The path wound among trees that reached up out of the dark earth from another world, like fingers groping, in search of light. On the ground, fallen branches of oak were strewn about like twisted limbs, shiny and brawny, every muscle plain to see in a macabre parody of mutilation, a battlefield strewn with fallen corpses - lying where they were slain. It made me uneasy and I quickened my pace, unwilling to linger among the Fairie folk.

The Bristol Channel was lying far below at the bottom of a ragged cliff. It glittered through the trees and blew in a sudden squall from the west that made the branches screech. A forked branch up in the canopy, too old and heavy to stay with mother, cracked and dropped towards earth, but was halted in its fall by stronger siblings. And there it stayed, suspended upside down like the Hanged Man of the Tarot, bearing silent witness to dark deeds. Imagined maybe, yet all too real to me.

There was a sound of dry twigs snapping in the leaf detritus deep within the wood. What could be making such a noise? In abject fear I peered through the trees, afraid of what I might see there. To my relief it was only deer, watching from a safe distance, skittish and cowardly. I hurried on with greater speed, now keeping close to the cliff edge, more exposed to the weather but in less danger from falling branches.

It was around lunchtime when I came upon Culbone Church.

It crossed my mind that this might be a good place to eat the sandwiches packed inside my rucksack, but I was neither hungry nor thirsty. Instead, I wandered round the church yard for a while, soaking up the peaceful atmosphere. The church was nestled in a wooded combe, and was the smallest church I had ever seen. After the fright in the woods, it felt like a place of sanctuary. An ancient Yew kept sentry duty, keeping the dead safe from the mischievous sprites in the woods.

The ground was littered with gravestones, most bearing the name of a local family. Annie Elisabeth Red, James Irving Red, Thomas Red; memorial stones covered in a peculiarly red lichen that was too red by far. I thought of ritual sacrifice and tombstones marinated in blood. As I stood, reading the messages of love and admiration, a sudden howling rose up from the forest, increasing in volume with every second. I have never heard the wail of a Banshee, but I swear that's what it was. I ran for the church and thanked a god I did not believe in that it was not locked against me.

Once inside, I checked the door to make sure the latch was safe in its housing. Whatever was out there needed to stay out there. It took a while for my eyes to become accustomed to the gloom. Uncomfortable looking box pews, of dark ancient wood, dominated the space, promising penance during prayers. A wooden screen formed a barrier between the congregation and the chancel, behind which were pillar candles resting on top of iron poles set on the floor, and an altar covered in lace. There was a strong scent of fresh lilies drifting through the musty air, mixed with a faint aroma of furniture polish. It was a comfort to know the Church was still in use and I hoped I would not be alone for long.

Suddenly, as if in response to that thought, the door began to rattle. Someone was trying to enter, struggling with the latch. I went to help but stopped when I saw a strange luminosity shining under the door. It was far too bright for sunlight. I backed away. On the other side of the windows, lights flickered and tiny fists banged on the leaden glass.

"Come away." A voice commanded. I swung my head round. There stood a vagrant, dressed in sack cloth and holding out a deformed hand.

"Come away. Leave the Fairie folk alone, they know nowt but mischief."

He must have seen the grimace on my face because he withdrew his hand and offered apology.

"Yer won't catch it. It's not catchin'. Them folk in Porlock think it so, but it's not. They won't allow us to cross Kil Beun water for fear we'll infect them fine folk that live there."

"Infect them with what?" I asked, concerned that whatever he had, I might catch it too. He ignored my question.

"All here work for cruel masters, they have no mind to keep us safe. We work hard for little pay until our fingers and toes drop off, then we crawl into the woods to die under the oak trees like wounded animals."

"How awful," I said, wanting to be kind, "What's your name?"

"I is Isaac. Came down from Kil Beun when the malady struck. I is a wood collier, work on the charcoal burners, hot, soulless work, none of sound body will do it." He waved his hands at me once more. This time I saw that most of the fingers were gone.

"Why are you here?" I said, thinking it an impertinent question but necessary to ask.

"When the weather turns bad, we go to the burning huts; they're of stone, good shelter. Sometimes we sleep there. I prefer here. I sleep more soundly, away from the Fairie. The masters beat us if they find us here, but it's worth a guinea's risk."

"You live here? In the middle of nowhere?"

"I has a rough shack up on Kitnor, built it meself from fallen oak branches, serves me well enough when the weather's fine. And we have food a plenty with the goats; milk and meat to feed us, skins to keep us warm when the sea winds bite."

That explained the aroma that had accompanied his appearance - a nauseating stench of male goat, mixed with rancid milk.

He came a step closer, "What business have you here Sire, with your strange attire and foreign talk?"

"There seems to have been a time slip," I said. He looked puzzled.

"Time? Slip? What means ye?"

"You're an apparition. A ghost from a time long gone."

The man rubbed his head with finger stumps. Dusty strands of hair fell over his eyes.

"I don't feel like a man gone to his grave," he said.

"There's no other explanation," I said.

"There is Sire. Maybe's you's the one who shouldn't be here. Maybe's you's the one who's slipped."

That was a thought to ponder. I had been feeling a little strange since my encounter at the Fairy Ring.

"What devilry is this?" An angry voice issued from the chancel as stern steps thundered down toward me, "Be-gone Son of Satan, for you cannot endure before the Lord."

I saw the hatchet before I saw the man, the hatchet wielded through the air with an agility that meant certain death for whomever it struck. There followed in its wake a man of tall stature dressed in a loosely fitting robe, tied at the waist with a soft strip of leather. A woollen cowl covered his head and shoulders.

"I see thee Albert of Esshe," he cried, "and I shall have thy head on a platter, like Herod did for our holy man of God, John the Baptist."

There followed a scream and a plea for mercy. The man who called himself Isaac was gone. In his place was a cowering lad of no more than fifteen years, bare-chested and wearing a loose cloth about his loins, gathered up between muscular legs and secured at the waist.

I'm not sure what valour possessed me but, without any thought at all, I placed myself between the hatchet and the boy.

"Stay thy hand," I commanded, wondering why I was talking that way.

"I shall not," the man raged, "It is my duty as Thomas, chaplain of Cattenor, to despatch this wickedness. Did I not vow before God to protect thee and thine?"

Now I was brought up a Methodist, so I knew the ten commandments off by heart. Not that I'd abided by them all you understand, though I'm sure coveting apples from a neighbour's garden is not that much of a sin anymore.

"Thou shalt not kill!" I yelled.

"The good prophet Moses also said Thou shalt not suffer a witch to live," he yelled back.

Pushing me aside with a strong arm that sent me reeling into the unyielding pews, he quickly despatched the poor boy with a blow to the head. It cracked his skull in two and left a gaping, bloody wound. I was furious and hell bent on retribution, man of the cloth or not. I reached out to take the hatchet from his murderous hand but all I found was air and a fading apparition.

"Come, come now," a soft voice said from the direction of the altar, "this way. We've seen the chapel, let us away to Embelle Wood, where I will show you Alph, the sacred river, that runs through caverns measureless to man, down to a sunless sea."

"Are you Samuel Coleridge!" I declared, "Well, well. Fancy meeting you here."

He turned to his companion, ignoring my address, "Do you know this impertinent fellow Wordy?"

"Indeed I do not Sammy," the man replied, "and I would say, it is not the crook who is to be feared most, it is the honest man who doesn't know what he is doing. Come, let us wander lonely as a cloud, that floats on high o'er vales and hills."

"Very good Wordy. I like that, you should use it in one of your poems."

With that they passed me by, giving wide berth, and left the church without lifting the latch.

"Pay no mind to them," it was Isaac, back from the dead, "nobody understands their ravings anyway. Pompous knaves."

"But how —"

"How come they be here? How come any of us be here? Tell me that! I was thinking on what you said, about slipping. Last I remember, I was curled up tight on a bed of bracken, fingers and toes all gone and no nose with which to smell the sea."

"You're dead then. Like I said,"

"You be dead too," Isaac replied without any trace of emotion, "We's all dead as far as I can tell."

It was then I remembered. The crumbling cliff overlooking the Bristol Channel. The signs warning of danger. One foot, just one foot, put wrong. Falling, bouncing against the sharp rocks on the way down, waiting for the impact, knowing it would be the end of me. And then the lights, flickering all around, tinkling with laughter, pulling me away to a place where spirits of bygone times are allowed free passage between the worlds.

Isaac was right. I was, most assuredly, dead.

*Afterword*

If you are ever passing Culbone Church, do please come inside. My companions and I will do our best to entertain you. If, however, the Fairie folk get to you first, rest assured you will be very welcome to join our little community.

*'Culled At Culbone'*

The Church of St Beuno at Culbone is the smallest church still in use in Britain. It is a mystical place, and was a sacred site even before the dawn of Christianity. Parts of the church date back to Saxon times.

The area around the church was once the site of a major charcoal burning industry. The original burners were lepers who were forbidden from crossing to the Porlock side of Culbone Water. Stone ruins marking the site of burners' huts can still be seen and there is a network of tracks connecting them to the main route through the woods. If you visit the church, look out for the lepers' squint hole in the north wall of the church. Feral goats lived here at that time and their milk, skins and meat were traded at Porlock Weir along with the charcoal.

It is believed that, around 1798, Samuel Taylor Coleridge came here with his friend William Wordsworth, and legend has it that the beautiful woodlands and coastal landscape provided the inspiration for some of their works. Indeed, nearby Embelle Wood is reputed to have been the inspiration for Coleridge's Xanadu in his most famous poem Kubla Khan.

As regards the murder in the church described in my story, it is recorded in the Assize Rolls of 1280 that Thomas, the chaplain of Cattenor (Culbone), was indicted 'for that he had struck Albert of Esshe (Ash) on the head with a hatchet, and so killed him.'

# Sacrilege At Sisters' Fountain

Out of the woods came an old man, looking care worn, skin wrinkled like leather. His companion, younger by at least three score years, was carrying a load heavy enough to make a packhorse weary.

"We will stop here a while," the old man said, "I'm in need of water and rest."

The younger man shrugged and made no answer. There was no water here but he was glad to lay his burden down for a while. He did not know where this man had come from, nor where he was bound. The accent was thick and strange, like nothing he had ever heard before. And he used unfamiliar words and did strange things with his hands, making signs to the wind and the birds and the clouds. All he carried was a wooden staff and a bundle of heavy sackcloth, which he clutched to his chest as if afraid someone might wrest it from his grasp. The young man had asked what manner of parcel this was for he fancied it may be the severed head of an enemy, or perhaps ancestral bones being returned to their homeland. The old man had answered by raising his eyes to the sky and muttering strange words that Jake, son of Ben, did not understand.

The place they had stopped was a secluded grove in the middle of dense woodland. Jake knew the ways of the forest and the creatures in it, and he knew that clearings like this could be dangerous. He warned the old man that they should not tarry long. In answer, the stranger had lifted up his staff, shouting again in his strange tongue, before bringing his staff crashing down onto the ground.

Straightway a spring burst forth, gushing water that drenched their feet.

Jake looked down at his sodden sandals, aghast. About to make comment on the miracle, he remembered how well he was being paid to escort this stranger from the coast and across the Somerset marshes - enough to buy food to see his family through the coming winter. So whatever manner of man this was, was no business of his and so he said not another word.

The old man cupped his hands in the water and drank his fill. Then, turning to Jake, he said, "We need to give thanks. Bring me a sacrificial lamb."

Now Jake had only ever hunted wild boar, for it was they who roamed the woodland hereabouts. He did not care to ask who they needed to thank but was sure that if he chopped off the head and skinned his catch the old man would be none the wiser. But he was ignorant of higher things and knew not the seriousness of his deception.

*                    *                    *

**Two thousand years later.**

The first time I saw him was on the path out of Minehead, just before the climb up to North Hill. He was wearing a rough jacket that hung loose without style. I noticed it particularly because it is not the sort of thing you see hikers wearing. And it looked dirty; he looked dirty: unwashed. We did not speak. He was in front of me but he must have heard me approaching because he glanced over his shoulder, saw me and then quickened his pace, putting more distance between us. Now I walk pretty fast but that morning I was thinking a bit slower than usual - I'd had a few beers the night before and it takes me a while to get going. I mention this just to show there couldn't have been anything wrong with him then. If there had been, he couldn't have kept up a pace like that. He was soon out of sight.

The next time I saw him was at Porlock Weir, some nine miles along the path. He was sat on the sea wall down at the harbour near The Anchor. Just sitting there. I guessed he was looking out at the fossilised stumps of trees on the beach. The tide was out you see and if you know what you're looking for, you can make them out. He must have been there quite some time because I'd stopped off in Porlock for coffee and cake. I always stop for elevenses. You need to keep sugar levels topped up on this path; it's a tough walk. Anyways, I walked on eventually overtaking him. I gave him a wide berth though - he stunk to high heaven. As I passed him, I couldn't help noticing what he had on his feet - not the sort of footwear you should wear on the South West Coast Path that's for sure. They were leather sandals, smelly looking things. And he had no socks on.

I carried on into Worthy Wood and, as I had already passed him, imagine my surprise when I saw him in front of me again. He was quite a bit ahead but I knew it was him because of his jacket. That's a bit odd, I thought. The guide book didn't say anything about any short cuts. Anyway, I pulled off the path shortly afterwards, heading for the road. I had booked into a Bed and Breakfast you see, for the night. I thought twelve miles was enough for one day.

Now that night, I had the strangest dream. In fact, it wasn't even like a dream; I felt like I was awake. You're going to think me daft, and I wouldn't normally mention this, but it is important to my story. I have never been religious and I don't believe in ghosts, don't even watch scary films, so this took me aback. It was dark in my bedroom, pitch black. There were no lights outside and none inside neither. As far as I knew, the lady who owned the house had gone to bed long before me and the house was quiet as a grave. When suddenly, there was a flash of light and I could see a figure standing in the corner of the room. And I swear to God it had wings. I thought it must be an angel, though like I say, I do not believe in all that stuff. But I felt it was trying to warn me about something. It said my name a few times, as though it was trying to tell me something but not managing it.

Needless to say, I did not sleep too well after that, so the following day, I was up early and set off before eight. I wanted to get to Lynmouth around noon, have some lunch, spend the afternoon there, browsing. Well I'll be damned if I didn't see the man in the dirty jacket again on the stretch of path that goes through the County Gate Nature Reserve. He stayed in front of me right the way to Coscombe. You have to cross a stream here and there is a signpost that tells you it is the boundary between Somerset and Devon. I tell you, he leapt over that stream like an elk: never hesitated, never faltered. Now me, well I took my time because I wanted to take a selfie with the sign in view. Not easy with short arms. After that I took a slight detour to find Sisters' Fountain. It was mentioned in the Guide Book and I thought it was worth a look, said it was where Joseph of Arimathea struck the ground with his staff to get water. I wondered if that's where my dream angel had come from, an imaginary figure I conjured up after reading all that religious mumbo jumbo the day before.

Anyway, at the time I was glad I had made the detour. I found a rocky mound of stone rubble, covered in moss and topped off with a stone cross. The spring comes out underneath and flows into a pool making for a very pleasant spot.

Well the place seemed deserted so I set my rucksack down, thinking I would have my elevenses here - though it was not even ten by that time but, as I said, I had set off early and was getting a bit peckish. I always carry a couple of chocolate bars - for emergencies - in case I don't happen on a cafe at the right time, so I took them out and settled myself down on the top, by the cross. It was drier up there. I had only taken one bite when I came over right queer. Can not explain it, I was just so tired, weary, like all the energy had drained from me. I leaned back against the cross, thinking I would have a little nap but, just at that moment, the man in the dirty jacket appeared from the woods. He was limping really badly and dragging a sack behind him. His mouth was moving like he was talking but nothing was coming out - I could not hear a thing. I don't know why but I thought it best not to let on I was there, so I kept quiet, hiding as best I could behind the stone cross. He came up really close and I held my breath in case I gave myself away. He had a most horrible wound on his leg, like he might have been bitten by a dog or caught in a hunter's trap. It was ragged raw and bleeding. I wondered if I should ask him what had happened but something stopped me. Call me a coward, or a hard bastard if you like, but I did not want to get involved. There was something about him, something not right. So I kept quiet and watched as he laid his sack down on the ground at the side of the pool before limping back into the woods.

Now the sack - well, it was bloodied like there might be something in it that I would not want to see, so I approached it a bit gingerly. In fact, I got a stick and poked it, trying to open it without touching it but I could not do it. I had to go right up to it and shake it out. And it took some doing, whatever was in there was mighty heavy and smelling rank. I did not need to get it all out, I could see as soon as the sack began to fall away what it was. It was a head, a boar's head. Well, I left it there, picked up my rucksack and ran. It freaked me out I can tell you. It was a strange business and no mistake. Fortunately, the man had gone off in the direction of Porlock so I was not likely to meet him again. I didn't hang about that's for sure.

It was only a few minutes later when I came upon the two stone pillars at the entrance to the Glenthorne estate - you know those with boars' heads on top. So I guessed that's what he'd been up to - poaching on private land. Though why he had a head in a sack is anybody's guess.

Well I passed through between the pillars, as the footpath sign directed, and a couple of minutes later I came upon a house, a chocolate box cottage with a red tiled roof and roses round the door, looking very quaint but very expensive at the same time. I could not help thinking of the cottage in the wood in the story of Hansel and Gretel. It was that sort of cottage - sugary and witchlike. There were brightly coloured flowers in window boxes and green herbs sprouting from the top of wall hung pots, fashioned like heads, with faces turned toward the doorstep. The windows were heavily leaded and draped in fancy, cream coloured lintels.

It was very pretty and I thought to take a photograph but just at that moment a face appeared at an upstairs window. I decided it would not be seemly to take a photo with the owner looking on, so I made to walk on. As I turned to go, I remembered the vision of the angel and felt a bit strange, like something wasn't right. But then the window was flung open and a woman shouted to me to go inside, said she needed help with moving something. Well, I have never denied a lady's request, and she was very pretty, so in I went.

"Come upstairs," she shouted, "Quickly now."

Well, I did not need telling twice. I fair leapt up those stairs two at a time, still with my rucksack on my back. I found her in the bedroom, standing by the window.

"Come," she said, "Don't be shy."

She was a good looking woman with long black hair and ice-blue eyes. Now I am not given to writing poems but the creamy skin of her cheeks, flushed with a soft peachy blush, brought all sorts of soppy lines to mind, and I could not help imagining what it would be like to kiss those plump red lips. I was almost salivating and no mistake.

"Are you strong?" she said as I approached. I told her I was, why I was Rochdale's boxing champion three years ago. She smiled when I said that.

"Then please remove this from my house," she was pointing to a sack on the floor, "You must take it to the spring on the hillside," she said, "it is an offering for the holy man who rests there."

Well my heart missed a beat. Actually I think it missed a few. It was the same sort of sack that the strange man had left behind.

"What's in it?" I asked.

"That's of no concern," she said, "I just want you to do as I ask."

She wasn't smiling when she said that, and it sounded a bit menacing, so I said, "Okay," and went to pick it up.

It was awfully heavy and I had to drag it over the carpet, across the landing and down the stairs. Once I got it outside, I noticed a red stain beginning to spread over the sacking, and the smell, well it was the same as the other sack, putrid like rotting flesh. It was then I decided I wanted no part of this and I dropped the sack by the gate. Well, she came flying down the stairs like she had wings on her feet. She was snarling and growling, lashing out with finger nails as big as talons. And her teeth! Oh my! Them were vampire teeth. She grabbed me by the legs and started gnawing and gnashing and spitting.

"Pick up the sack," she said, hissing the words through her bloodied teeth, "and take it to the holy ground, or I'll eat you alive."

Well, I didn't need telling twice. I don't know how I dragged myself and the sack all the way to Sisters' Fountain, but I did.

When I got there, I found an old man with a grey beard, dressed in a long, mud-stained robe and carrying a wooden staff. I dropped the sack at his feet and turned to make my escape.

"What manner of lamb is this?" he yelled. I explained as best I could that I thought it was a wild boar and I told him who had made me bring it. That made him really angry and he started shouting about cloven hooves and desecration of holy ground. He shook his staff at me and cursed me, told me he was going to cast me down to Hell.

Next news I am up here, on Desolation Point with the man in the dirty jacket. He tells me his name is Jake, son of Ben, says he has been up here a long time. We are sitting together on the headland watching the setting sun, waiting for our transport. Something tells me he won't be needing his jacket where we're going.

*'Sacrilege At Sisters' Fountain'*

The spring at Sisters' Fountain is reputed to have come into existence when Joseph of Arimathea struck the ground with his staff. Having landed at Looe in Cornwall he was on his way to Glastonbury, carrying the Holy Grail.

The cross was erected above the spring in the 19th century by the owner of Glenthorne Estate, naming it Sisters' Fountain because the area was a playground for his nieces.

# No More Fun On The Funicular

*'A trip to the picturesque towns of Lynton and Lynmouth is not complete without a ride on the famous funicular rail.'*

That is what the advertising literature said. It also said;

*'The Water Powered Lift is the best and most exciting way to travel between these historic towns and will be one of the highlights of the day - for Mums, Dads and all the family.'*

And that was true. For over a hundred years, tourists had been gliding up and down the cliff, savouring their ice cream whilst admiring the stunning views over Exmoor and the North Devon coastline. Built by Victorian engineers, it seemed indestructible. It had even survived the cataclysmic floods of 1952. Sadly, the recent accident changed everything.

Twenty five people died, including six children. It was initially reported that the brakes had failed but it was not true. There were four separate braking systems, all working independently so if it had been faulty brakes, they would all have had to fail at the same time. The families who had lost loved ones were promised compensation, of course, but all they really wanted was someone to blame.

"These things don't just happen," one of them said on National News, "the world works on cause and effect. Someone or something caused this terrible accident and we want to know exactly who and what it was."

Witnesses said that the cars had seemed to explode when they crashed into the docking stations but this fact was either ignored or over-looked by the authorities. In the mind of the Council Investigating Officer, explosion meant terrorism and who the heck would want to blow up a few tourists in Lynmouth? Besides, forensics had checked for incendiaries and nothing had been found.

The official line went something like this:

*'When the cars are 'docked' the tank of the top car is filled with water from the River Lyn until the cars are in balance. When loaded with passengers, the drivers use bell signals to tell each other when to unlock the safety device that controls the brakes. The lower driver then discharges water to make the top car heavier, causing the top car to roll down the rails - at the same time pulling up the lower car. What happened in this case was that too much water was discharged from the lower car causing both cars to move at too great a speed and crash into the docking stations, which then jettisoned the cars and their passengers.'*

The drivers protested loudly at the implication that they had been at fault, either by discharging too much water or by misinterpreting the bell signal. They blamed the engineers, the engineers blamed the maintenance team and the maintenance team blamed the design. Eventually, all agreed that both the brakes, and the water discharge system, had most likely malfunctioned due to microscopic debris having become lodged inside the mechanism in the recent heavy rain. Although no evidence was found for this, it was concluded that it would not have been visible on a routine inspection and so no one was to blame. The explosions, that witnesses had reported when the cars hit the docking stations, were never mentioned.

Graham Davies, PhD., retired Professor of Molecular Hydrodynamics, (that's a man who knows all there is to know about water), had a very good idea about what had caused the accident and he went to see the Investigation Team.

"It's the water," he said, "There is something in the rain."

But they wouldn't listen to him, probably thought he was just another ageing academic, bored with his retirement, and possibly in the first stages of dementia.

The trouble with the Professor was that he was quietly spoken, hesitant in speech and every inch an academic. Which usually meant he would lose his listeners before he'd even reached the end of his first sentence. He was acutely aware of his effect on people and did try very hard to be eloquent and interesting. But he knew the signs all too well - as soon as the eyes glazed over, his listener would drift away, if not in body, then in mind.

Having been dismissed by the Council, he took his story to the local paper, but they wouldn't listen either. That was a shame because the tragedy of the funicular railway was just the start. Things were about to get pretty weird.

His suspicion that there was something in the rain had been aroused three weeks before the accident when he discovered, what appeared to be, a self-replicating catalyst in the rain water butt in his garden. He had gone out to get water for his indoor plants and had noticed, with surprise, that the water level in the butt was going down despite the endless rainy days. He had taken a sample of the water and carried out some basic investigations in his kitchen. These showed that whatever was in there was, as he phrased it in his journal, 'eating the water'. With only a portable centrifuge and a few test tubes, he had managed to isolate a non-biological substance that appeared to be catalysing the reaction that was making the water disappear. That sent him running to his old University to borrow research equipment surreptitiously that would help him look further into this strange phenomenon. What he found was quite bizarre.

The catalyst was being carried by a viral vector and was breaking the hydrogen bonds in the water, releasing the hydrogen and oxygen atoms into the air. He checked the replication time of the virus. It was very slow, especially in the low winter temperatures. When the accident occurred, he theorised that the water in the funicular tanks must have been warmed by friction, which would then allow the vector, with its lethal cargo, to speed up its replication process. He suspected that the resulting release of highly flammable hydrogen was responsible for the explosions. The trouble was, it was a difficult concept to explain to the uninitiated and he did not have any tangible evidence - all he had was his journal notes.

The team who had investigated the accident reported that there was nothing wrong with the water that was driving the hydraulic pistons, apart from the fact that there seemed to be a lack of it. Of course, if they had been scientists and had known what to look for, it would have been a different story. Unfortunately, municipal organisations do not deal with the impossible. Any answer will do providing it sounds plausible, however improbable.

In the days following the accident, the Professor stepped up his research. After only a week he observed that the water in his experimental tank was disappearing at an ever increasing rate, even though the tank had a continuous and endless supply of water. That could only mean that there was more catalyst than before.

The following week, the rate of water disappearance became alarming, almost instantaneous. It was clear that something else had been thrown into the mix, especially as the water now seemed to be intermittently vibrating of its own accord.

That sent him back to the University where he cajoled a lab technician in the Department of Physics to loan him a vibration analyser. This instrument, carefully secured to the roof of his garage, detected a massive source of vibrational energy being beamed from a satellite in orbit around the earth, passing over Lynmouth every four hours. The vibration was so strong that the atoms in the water were being shaken apart every time the satellite passed overhead. He also noticed that the hydrogen was now miraculously disappearing as soon as it was released from the water, it was just vanishing. The oxygen, on the other hand, was simply dissipating into the surrounding air. Graham knew that if this were to happen on a large scale, it would result in a worrying increase of oxygen in the atmosphere.

He took his findings to one of his old research colleagues at the University. She was about to fly off to Brazil for a conference, but promised to look through the data on her return.

*            *            *

**At No. 10 Downing Street.**

The Managing Director of A.E.S. (Alternative Energy Sources) felt very uncomfortable. He had been summoned to Downing Street for a meeting with the Prime Minister, the Energy Secretary and the Environment Minister.

"I'm sorry," the Managing Director said, "There's nothing more we can do. It's beyond our control." His report was not what the Government wanted to hear.

"Oh dear," commented the Environment Minister, who had an overly extended forehead that was furrowed like a newly ploughed field, "Looks like we've messed up again."

"We've spent a lot of money funding this project," the Prime Minister interjected, "we need it to work. There's an election due."

"Oh it works alright," the MD replied, "works too well as it happens."

"How can it work too well?" the PM was beginning to sound impatient, he had no time for obtuse insinuations, "I want facts, not clever quips. We need all the free energy we can get our hands on."

“It’s a chain reaction,” the MD explained, “We had stringent containment regulations in place but they took no account of epigenetic mutations.”

The Prime Minister looked confused by this new revelation. He had no idea what the man was talking about. The Environment Minister, however, turned the colour of puce,

“You mean the vector carrying the catalyst has mutated and escaped into the environment?”

“I’m afraid so,” the MD said, his head now resting on his chest to avoid any further eye contact.

The Energy Secretary who was sitting at the far end of the table raised her eyebrows, “Why is that a problem?” she said, “The technology we have is already mopping up the released hydrogen. We cannot have enough of it. After all, it’s the only energy source we have left.”

The MD got to his feet, it was time for him to leave. “Somehow,” he said, “I don’t think we’ll be around to make use of it.”

*   *   *

**Two weeks later**

“Channel Four News, Professor Davies. May I speak with you a moment?”

Graham Davies pretended not to hear the request. He was running down to the promenade and didn’t want to be delayed. He had had word that something strange was going on and he wanted to see for himself. The man kept pace with him, a huge fluffy microphone bouncing along beside him. There was a television crew in close pursuit.

The man with the microphone persisted, "Can you tell us something about what you think might be going on? I understand you have a theory about this?"

Graham still did not answer. It was all he could do to keep breathing. With all the research he had been doing lately he had had no time to keep up his exercise regime. At last Lynmouth promenade came into view and he came to a halt so suddenly that the cameraman narrowly avoided running into him.

"That my friend is what's going on," he said, panting noisily.

There were more than a dozen people on Blacklands Beach and they were all coughing and spluttering, some falling down, clutching their chest. A woman in a red jacket was shouting for help. A child lay convulsing at her feet, its face turning the same colour as her jacket. On the promenade, an elderly gentleman staggered as he steered his wife toward a wooden bench. They both collapsed before they got there.

"Get everyone off the beach," Graham yelled, "Get off the beach."

"Why?" the TV man wanted to know, "What's happening?"

"The air," Graham yelled; it was hard to hear his own voice above the pandemonium, "There's too much oxygen. It's poisoning them."

A man nearby began shouting through a loud hailer,

"Everyone off the beach, get as far away from the shore as you can."

Police sirens joined the orchestra of ambulance sirens as people ran or crawled onto the promenade, some carrying their unconscious loved ones with them.

Graham rushed over to where a Paramedic was administering oxygen to a man lying on the ground.

"Don't do that," he shouted, "You'll kill him."

The Paramedic ignored him and began to speak into his lapel microphone,

"Pain in the chest - difficulty breathing - must be an air-borne toxin. We need to get these people to hospital."

"It's pulmonary oxygen toxicity," Graham insisted, kneeling on the ground beside the medic who was now checking for a pulse, "The sea's releasing oxygen; there's too much in the air."

"Leave it to the professionals, pal," the Paramedic said, pushing him away.

"He's having a seizure," Graham yelled, snatching the oxygen mask away, "get him to hospital."

Suddenly, there was an ear splitting noise like a thousand thunder-claps all happening at the same time. Graham looked towards the beach. The sea was starting to boil and bubble like soup in a cauldron. A thick layer of white mist was forming above the surface, filled with lightning flashes and explosions.

He turned back to the Paramedic who was still trying to resuscitate the man on the ground,

"It's too late for him," he said, "It's too late for all of us."

*'No More Fun On The Funicular'*

The railway, or cliff lift as it is sometimes known, was opened on Easter Monday in 1890. It has two cars, each capable of transporting forty passengers, and requires two drivers for its operation. The cars are joined by a continuous cable running around a pulley at each end of the incline. It is entirely independent of any power apart from water, which feeds through pipes from the West Lyn River over a mile away into tanks under the floor of the upper car. During operation, water is discharged from the lower car until the heavier top car begins to descend under gravity, with the speed controlled by a brakeman travelling on each car. A large water accumulator provides the force to keep the brakes permanently locked on until manually released by the drivers using bell signals to communicate with each other. To stop at the station the drivers gently apply the brakes and lower the bottom car onto the buffers.

For those of you not inclined to ride the funicular after reading my story, be assured that in the event of too much water being released by the drivers, the speed of the cars is restricted by a failsafe mechanism.

The Lynmouth flood conspiracy theory should also have mention. After the devastating floods of 1952 there was speculation (which is still going on today) that the flooding was caused by experimentation in cloud seeding. This is a form of weather modification that works by dispersing substances into the air that serve as nuclei to which water vapour can attach, forming rain clouds.

# Devilry On Rawn's Rocks

This is another story with an unhappy ending - though worse than the others because it is true. If I were you, I would go and buy yourself a popular magazine and escape into a cacophony of celebrity tittle tattle so you won't have to think about the awful implications of what I am about to reveal.

This story tells the truth about death, your death, my death, everybody's death, and I am about to tell you that death is a very unhappy ending, no matter what you do in life, no matter how good you think you've been.

The things I am about to relate had such an impact on me that I have become like Coleridge's Ancient Mariner, re-telling my story to everyone I meet. I have even put it on Facebook and would not be surprised if it ends up an urban myth like the alligators in the New York sewers or the cryogenically frozen body of Walt Disney. The difference is, of course, that this is not a myth. It happened and it is going to happen to you. And no matter how great your disbelief, somewhere deep inside, you will know that your life will end this way.

I could begin my revelation by telling you that I discovered this great truth a long time ago on a cold, dark mid-winter night when the moon was full. That would make it a more acceptable tale, less real. But I cannot say that because it is not true and all I am interested in is telling you the truth. I am compelled to tell my story the way it really happened. And the way it happened was this.

It was the Day of the Dead, but I was nowhere near Oaxaca – not even in Mexico. I was in North Devon, on the summit of Great Hangman to be precise. It was unseasonably warm for the end of October. I'd gone up there with a friend, Ollie, but he only got halfway up and had to back track. He suffers from asthma and did not have his inhaler. I carried on without him, eager to see the view from the top.

I reckon it was when I was approaching the cairn that I felt it. A presence. I could not explain it but I felt like I was being watched. I thought to shrug the feeling off and sat down on the stones, got my flask out and poured a well earned cup of coffee, accompanied by a Garibaldi. That is when I saw something - but, whatever it was, disappeared in an instant. It was noon, in full sunlight, there were no shadows, so it couldn't have been that.

I did what anybody would have done and put it down to imagination. I finished my coffee and biscuit, took a few photographs and was just packing up my rucksack when a man approached from the direction of Little Hangman. I remember he was sweating profusely. Being rather rotund and looking quite out of condition, he must have found the climb up the Hangman very challenging. Once he had got his breath, we discussed the weather, as we English have a tendency to do. He was a pleasant chap and we swapped comments about the view and the calmness of the sea. He pointed out Lundy Island and the coast of South Wales and told me some interesting sea faring tales from the time when Combe Martin was a busy sea port. He said these cliffs we were standing on, were full of manganese and silver that were traded for coal from the Welsh mines.

He also mentioned Rawn's Rocks, said there had been some funny goings on there lately. When I asked what he meant, he suddenly changed, almost like Jekyll and Hyde. His eyes went sort of glazed and he seemed to look right through me. He started swearing, told me I was a nosy - well I will not repeat the word he used - accused me of spying on him. Well, I did not know what to say so I turned away, thinking to head back down the hill toward Sherrycombe. Then I heard him scream, a sort of horrible, gurgling scream like he was drowning. That is when I saw it again. It was crouched over him, oozing and flowing like chocolate sauce over a suet pudding.

Well I started to run I can tell you. Anybody would have done the same. By the time I found Ollie, I was a dithering wreck. I told him what had happened and he said we should call the police.

"And tell them what?" I said, "That a man's been killed by a black slithering monster?"

He offered to go up and look but with his asthma, said he didn't want to chance it. So he called the police. Give them their due, they were there in no time considering we were a long way from any roads. Brought the coast guard and an ambulance crew with them as well and we all walked back up the Hangman together, even Ollie - he was gasping and complaining mind you but said he didn't want to miss out on the excitement.

We found the man lying just where he had been when the black oozy thing had smothered him. But there was no sign of anything untoward. The Paramedic pronounced him dead and said it looked likely he had had a heart attack - being overweight and all. I tried to tell them about the black thing but they gave me an amused look and asked what I had been drinking.

After they had packed the man up in a body bag and carted him off, Ollie and I sat on the sprawling cairn and talked about what I had seen. He was making excuses. It was probably a shadow, perhaps I was tired and had hallucinated? Had it been a dog? I was getting exasperated with him, getting myself in a right stew, when suddenly I saw it again. It was oozing up the hill towards us.

I screamed. I could not speak so I pointed. Ollie looked and said he could not see anything. Next news it is on him and he is gurgling and crying out just like the other man. I could not run away, not this time, could not leave my friend like that. But what could I do? I just watched in horror as Ollie breathed his last, clutching at his throat. But it meant I got a good look at it this time. It was not solid, it was more like thick black smoke from burning rubber. It even smelled bad. I would call it a stench rather than a smell, (think of rotting meat mixed with old fish skins). 'It' looked right at me, yes it had eyes, but they weren't like any eyes I have ever seen before. They were burning red with black pupils that wavered and oscillated. It had no other features and yet I felt it was smiling at me. And then it spoke,

"I am death," it said, "Know me for I will come for you in five years, three months, two days, eight hours and twenty three minutes."

And then it was gone and my friend was dead. And I had to call the police back. And they arrested me, said it all looked a bit suspicious. I even started to wonder it myself. It did seem a bit of a coincidence and with me hearing voices and everything. They even brought in a forensic psychiatrist but in the end I was released because of a lack of evidence and no obvious motive. Between you and me, I think the police thought I was some sort of psychopath.

*          *          *

It has been over five years since those incidents on Great Hangman and I've seen the thing on many occasions since then, and it always takes a life away. So it cannot be me. I see lots of them on the television, all crowding together in the war zones, oozing over the poor people caught in those terrible conflicts. I do not think they kill people, I do not think they can do that, but they take the souls, carry them off somewhere.

One of them took my father last month. I was with him when it came but there was nothing I could do except hold his hand and mutter words of comfort and reassurance - all lies of course, but you cannot tell someone the truth on their deathbed.

The Crematorium garden has a huddle of large boulders near the entrance and, for some reason, the sight of them caused me to remember what the man on the Hangman had said about there having been funny goings on at Rawn's

Rocks. I rushed home right after the funeral to Google them but found nothing except that they were laid down as desert sand almost four hundred million years ago and then raised up by the movement of the earth beneath. I had a mental image of them being spewed up from the bowels of Hell, an image so vivid I could have been seeing the actual event. That did it. I had to go there and see for myself.

I booked a B & B in Combe Martin knowing full well it might be the last holiday I would ever take. I cannot deny I was full of trepidation about what I might find. I think I was hoping to find an answer, a way out, a stay of execution perhaps.

It took me a while to find the rocks and when I did, I could not get onto them, the footing was far too dangerous. Not that I would have wanted to, not after what I saw there. It turned my blood cold. The rocks were covered in hundreds of the little black devils, squirming and squealing, seeping and shrieking. It was as though the rocks themselves were giving birth to these monsters. Some of them were sliding into the water and swimming away, others were taking to the air, flying away like a murmuration of starlings at dusk.

I could hear them talking, whispering on the sea breeze, "We are everywhere," they said, "In your dreams, in your mind, multiplying, overcoming. Ready to claim what was promised us."

I will never forget those words as long as I draw breath. I have never been very religious but the time foretold me is fast approaching. The moment I got home I went to see the Vicar at my local church, but he just smiled sympathetically and told me not to worry. He would not have smiled if he had seen what I had seen hovering at the hem of his vestment. That sent me running to Father Dermot at St. Damien's. He told me to repent my sins and commit to Christ but I could see the things hiding under the pews, biding their time. I went to see an Imam in the town's Mosque but they were there too, running round in plain sight. The Jewish temple, the Christian Science Meeting Hall, the Evangelists, the Methodists, the Rastafarians, the Congregationalists and the Buddhists - none of them were free of the abominable things.

* * *

So, my tale is almost at an end. When I began, I had twenty minutes left, I now have only three. Fear has me girdled like a hangman's noose. The terror I feel I cannot tell. A black devil is close by. I can see him. He keeps turning away, pretending he is looking for someone else, but I know it is me he wants. What will happen to me after he has sucked out my soul? Will I hover above my lifeless body, wondering what will happen next? Will I find myself in some hellish torment?

I pray to God to save my soul but all I hear in reply is Don McLean singing;

*And the three men I admire most,*
*The Father, Son and the Holy Ghost,*
*They caught the last train for the coast,*
*The day, the music died . . .*

*'Devilry On Rawn's Rocks'*

Great Hangman is the highest sea cliff in England and the highest point on the South West Coast Path. It lies, alongside Little Hangman, just north of Combe Martin where Exmoor meets the sea.

No early forms of the place-name *Hangman* are recorded. It was first mentioned in 1792 as *Hangman Hill*. The name is probably a mixture of Celtic and Germanic languages, giving a literal translation of 'sloping hill', (Wikipedia). However, local legend has a far more interesting theory. It seems a sheep stealer, with a stolen ewe slung over his shoulder, stopped to rest on the hillside. He had tied a cord around the sheep's legs and, as it began to struggle, the cord tightened and somehow slipped around the man's neck, strangling him.

# Nightmare In Appledore

The telephone was ringing but Liz had decided not to answer it. She was curious to know how that felt and discovered it felt quite good - made her feel she was back in control of her life. The fact that she did not feel like talking to anyone just now had nothing to do with it. This was all about reclaiming her personal power.

It never occurred to her that the call might be important.

She turned up the volume on the radio.

*"We sweat and laugh and scream here, 'cause life is just a dream here . . . hey, hey."*

For some reason, the screaming tones of Alice Cooper made her heart beat faster, stirring the familiar feeling of anxiety and causing the vague memory of a forgotten dream to creep out of the shadows of her mind.

*"Yeah, welcome to my nightmare . . ."*

She had woken in the night, feeling abandoned and desolate, from a nightmare too horrific to be remembered. Was the DJ playing this song just for her, so she would remember? That was a crazy thought; just a temporary return of the paranoia - a glitch in the system, ghosts in the machinery. Picking up the remote, she pressed the red button and Alice Cooper fell silent. It was not normal to think like this but the doctor had warned her that recovery might be slow. Perhaps it was the upset over Angela yesterday. Angela had let her down at the last minute again because Angela always had more important things to do, more important people to see. This time it was something about having to administer emergency healing to one of her clients. Never mind about her. What was important was how she felt. Being let down always catapulted her back into that horrible, self-pitying state that she had been fighting so hard to stay out of; the sort of state that stopped her sleeping and drove people away.

She had moved here last year with a dream of a new life, abandoning an abusive partner for new friends, happier times. But the new friends had not materialised - except for Angela who had found her crying in the park one day. Probably felt sorry for her. Angela was that sort of person. A good person. The person Liz would like to be. Sometimes they went down to The Beaver for a drink but it was always full of arty types and Liz felt out of place. Once she had gone down on her own but had hidden away in a corner, waiting for an opportunity to leave unnoticed. People back home had asked her why she had moved here without checking things out first. The truth was that she had been intoxicated with the quaint charm of the place and thought that would be enough.

She had bought a house out in the sticks, up on Long Lane. It had been empty for over a year so she had managed to negotiate a good price, but living up here, over a mile from the quay, she had found herself isolated and alone. And the nightmares were not helping. She had had bad dreams before, lots of them, but never nightmares, and the one last night was the worst ever. Angela had said there was something not right about the house, but that was just Angela. She had wanted to do a cleansing ceremony but that was too weird and Liz had refused. The thought of Angela going from room to room, ringing a bell and splashing salt water around was enough to give her even more nightmares.

What she needed was some fresh air in the April sunshine. A stroll down to the quay was the ticket, get some chocolate and maybe buy a DVD from the charity shop. They usually had a nice assortment of films with happy endings; they were the medications that did not need a prescription. She loved wandering around Appledore with its narrow streets running straight as arrows down to the quay, with the little alleyways between them. If the sun stayed out perhaps she would walk across the burrows to Westward Ho! She might even buy some apples and feed the horses that grazed there.

Grabbing her coat and purse, she made for the door, glancing back at the telephone. For a moment she thought it was going to ring again, but it didn't.

*　　　　*　　　　*

Inspector Reinhart wasn't unduly worried. If she was not answering the telephone then she probably was not at home, and if she was not at home then she wasn't in any danger. The Prison Doctor was adamant that Kelly would return to the scene of the crime. Damn the parole board. Kelly had served ten years of his life sentence when the board decided, in their infinite wisdom, to let him loose on society. They said he was cured of the pathological condition that had driven him to murder a young woman and traumatise her four year old daughter, said he was ready to be given a second chance. Who the hell had they been kidding? Four days out of prison and he had disappeared. His probation officer had been found half an hour ago on a rubbish tip with his throat cut.

"Better send a couple of cars round to the house," Reinhart said to his second in command, "In the meantime, keep trying the phone."

Leaving his staff to get on with their assigned tasks, he made his way along a windowless corridor that led to the interview rooms. The walls were painted a pale green because some psychologist in the 1980s had decided it was a restful colour that would keep the arrested scum and lowlife, calm. He knocked on the door at the end and entered without waiting to be invited in. A teenage girl was sitting in an easy chair, hands clasped together on her knees, looking tense. An older woman, a police counsellor, was sitting opposite her, brought in from a neighbouring force because Inspector Reinhart was not as diplomatic as circumstances demanded. He nodded to the woman to continue as he settled himself into a less comfortable chair at the back.

"I know this is hard for you Cassie," the police counsellor said in a voice that Reinhart thought was too soft, almost patronising, "but we need you to tell us everything you can remember about that day."

"How could I ever forget?" the girl said, "it's not that long since I stopped having nightmares about it."

"How old were you? Four?"

The girl nodded.

"The file says you weren't interviewed at the time. There was enough evidence for a conviction and, you were so young, the police didn't want to put you through that."

Inspector Reinhart was watching for the girl's reaction. He knew the counsellor would stop the interview if she became distressed.

"So why now?" Cassie asked, "Why drag it all up again?"

The woman took hold of the girl's hand and squeezed it gently,

"He's been released Cassie. On parole."

"Released! Released!" she screamed.

"Try and keep calm," the woman said, "the police will catch him."

Turning round to face Reinhart, she added, "Won't you Inspector?"

"We'll catch him, Cassie," the Inspector said with more conviction than he was feeling.

"He's still mentally ill," the woman continued, "and the Forensic Psychologist thinks he might return to the house to re-enact his crimes. You understand how important this is, don't you?"

"We need to know exactly what his moves will be," Reinhart said, "how he'll get into the house for instance, so we can protect the family that lives there now."

Cassie began to cry.

"I know this is difficult Cassie," the woman said, "But don't let what happened to you and your mother happen to someone else."

"We were making a cake," Cassie said, "I remember that because Mum had shouted at me for dropping the eggs on the floor. We had to go down to the shop to get some more, you see it was my fault. If I hadn't broken the eggs we would never —"

"You can't blame yourself for what happened," the woman interrupted gently, "You were just a little girl."

"He just appeared behind us," Cassie said, "I don't know where he came from, he was just suddenly there. He had a knife and he got hold of me and dragged me back to the house. Mum was running after us, screaming."

"You mean he was waiting for you in the lane?" the Inspector asked.

Cassie nodded and began to sob uncontrollably.

Inspector Reinhart left the room. The counsellor could comfort the girl, he had more important things to do.

* * *

Liz's thoughts were far away from the black mood that had driven her out of doors. As she walked down the lane she breathed in the sweet scent of the spring air, filled with the mating calls of birds returning home for the summer. Approaching the point where Long Lane turns into Torridge Road, the great sand flats of the estuaries where the Rivers Taw and Torridge meet came into view on her left, the rivers reflecting the brilliant blue of the sky. It was then that she became aware of footsteps behind her. Glancing briefly over her shoulder, she was a little surprised to see a man she did not recognise. You did not see many strangers round here out of season, especially not up here in Watertown. Thinking nothing more of it, and not wanting to appear rude by staring at the man, she turned her head back and carried on walking.

"Where's the kid?" an asthmatic voice demanded.

Liz was startled and turned again to face the stranger.

"I beg your pardon?" she said.

"The kid. Where is she?"

"What kid?"

"Your kid Missus." The man spat, "The one you had with you before."

Liz noticed the spittle on his parched, purple lips and felt a coldness creeping over her. The blackness of the dream was approaching and Alice Cooper began singing inside her head,

*'Welcome to my breakdown. I hope I didn't scare you.'*

"I don't know what you mean." She stammered.

The man pulled a knife from under his jacket. She started to run but he lurched forward and grabbed her arm, pulling her to his chest. The sunlight lit up the fine detail of the knife. An enamelled shield, carefully worked in green and red, was embedded into the black handle. She saw all its intricate detail. At the hilt of the blade there was an engraved cross and the words, memento mori, emblazoned across it. A disembodied voice screamed the translation in her head, *remember you will die*.

The next moment she had fallen into an incomprehensibly vast, empty space, a rippling void of darkness, seeking her out, suffocating her. It was inside her, bloating her with terror, blowing her up like a balloon, embracing her from within with its horror of emptiness.

*'Welcome to my Nightmare. . .'* Alice Cooper again; sounding triumphant. Now she remembered the dream, and this was it, replaying in every detail.

“No, no,” she yelled, lashing out, scratching and kicking, “You’re a dream, you can’t hurt me.”

And then she was above the lane, hovering, looking at herself crumpled like a rag doll on the tarmac. Her assailant was lying face down at her side, held by two police officers who were cuffing him.

* * *

“How is she, Doctor?” asked Inspector Reinhart.

“Not good.” The Doctor answered as he pulled up a chair.

“You got to her just in time, Inspector. A few minutes later and —” the Doctor stopped mid-sentence and gesticulated across his throat, “Anyway, she has no physical injuries apart from broken finger nails and a few cuts to the neck. Psychologically however . . .”

The Inspector cast him a questioning glance.

“She's showing all the signs of REM atonia, that's when the brain awakens from a rapid eye movement state but the body is unable to move. The technical term is hallucinatory sleep disorder, though it is usually transient, lasting for no more than a few seconds. It's a frightening state to be in.”

“You mean she's dreaming?”

“In a way, yes,” the Doctor was picking his words carefully, “She's unaware of anything going on around her and yet she's certainly seeing and experiencing something. We can tell that because she’s showing all the signs of a night terror; you know, eyes open, arms flaying. She’ll believe she’s awake and is no doubt suffering all the symptoms of this state; feeling there’s a kind of demonic presence trying to attack her. This will be very real to her.”

The Inspector looked grave as the doctor continued, "I think she believes she died out there and all her physical senses have somehow been switched off."

"Will she recover?" the Inspector asked with genuine concern.

The Doctor shrugged, "The mind is still largely uncharted territory Inspector. We'll do our best of course, we have all manner of treatments at our disposal, but she's not responding."

"Will she ever?" the Inspector was thinking of his own daughter, about the same age and living alone.

"Our last resort will be to put her into an induced coma," the doctor said, "trouble is, we've no idea whether or not that will stop the nightmare she's caught in. I think, whatever we do, she's going to have to find her own way out of it."

* * *

The rain had started again, lashing down in a torrent that blurred Liz's vision and hid her attacker from view. It turned the lane to mud and she cursed it as she slipped and stumbled down to the village. The Post Office was closed. Why was it closed? It should be open. She banged on the door,

"Let me in," she screamed. "Help me."

No one answered and the door remained shut against her. She could hear the voice of a man calling her name, softly at first and then screaming it in her ear. He took hold of her, intending to carry her off. He meant to harm her. She wrenched herself free and ran down to the seashore, across the rocks and into a wide, open desert where hot sand shimmered under a relentless sun, a no man's land. She slowed her pace, her legs becoming heavier until she could barely move. A black dog appeared on the horizon, held on a leash by a man with long, dirty hair and dressed in black leather. He was laughing and screaming at her,

"Welcome to my nightmare Liz . . ."

They came closer, the dog was snarling, trying to bite her. The man pointed towards the cliffs where dark beings, his allies, were waiting for her.

"You know you feel right at home here inside my nightmare," he said with a sly smile.

She turned away. There was a wood in the distance and a clear path, well tended, snaking through the trees. She was there in no time but then ravens came and hid the path, and brambles scratched at her body. She could see shadows hiding in the branches of tall trees and a river before her, deep and fast flowing. On the opposite bank was a small hut, with a welcoming light in the window. Logs floated by, inviting her to step aboard, but some of them had jaws like crocodiles and large green eyes that watched her. Someone shouted from the depths of the forest,

"Liz, come back."

Another voice called from the doorway of the hut, "What a lovely surprise. But you can't stay sweetheart." It was a voice she recognised, a voice from long ago. It was the voice of her Grandmother.

"Come back," the voice from the forest again. "Come away from the light."

"Help me cross the river," she cried to her Grandmother, but there was no answer and the light in the hut faded until all light was gone, leaving only darkness and the horrors that it hid. She turned back to the forest; the blackness, palpable and stenching, turned with her. A man was approaching. She recognised him; it was Alice Cooper and he was singing,

*"Welcome to my nightmare, woo, hoo...Welcome to my breakdown..."*

She ran to the water but mud, as slippery as ice, was under her feet and she felt herself falling, falling, deeper into the black water. She could not breathe. It was in her lungs. She tried to scream. And then a face, radiant, loving, and a hand with a gentle touch was pulling her, lifting her up.

"Liz . . . dreaming . . . come back . . . Liz."

Her eyes fluttered open. Glaring lights. Noise. Distant chattering. A smell of disinfectant in the air. A canula in her arm. And Angela, dear, dear Angela, called out to another emergency.

*'Nightmare In Appledore'*

The name Appledore is probably Celtic in origin and was the site of a Saxon settlement, becoming an important port in Elizabethan times. It is situated at the mouth of the River Torridge.

When I passed through it on my journey along the South West Coast Path I was captivated by its charm. It is such a pretty place I just could not resist giving it a counter-balancing dark side.

***The author signing the visitors' book inside Ronald Duncan's hut.***

# Picnic At Embury Beacon

It was a day for doing nothing, a day set aside to enjoy the sweet rewards of a father and daughter reunion.

They had had an early start and had begun the day by walking southward along the coast path to check out Ronald Duncan's hut, which was perched on the headland just above Marsland Mouth. Ella's father had told her he had always wanted to be a writer and he had looked very much the part as he sat himself down at Duncan's old worn desk.

"What a wonderful place to summon the literary muse," he had said, "a boundary, a crossing over place. Here we are in Devon, yet looking out over Cornwall."

She had taken a photograph of him sitting there, hoping that it would be a sweet reminder of them crossing their boundary of silence.

"If I'd had a place like this, how different things might have been," he had said.

She did not know how things had been for him, she only knew how things had been for her. And she did not want to ask him and spoil this magical time together. She hoped there would be plenty of time for questions, for the awkwardness, for the excuses. Plenty of time to rake over the past. As it was she was content to watch him, listen to him and pretend they had never been apart. Her father meant a lot to her. In truth, he was all she had.

They were back at the car well before lunchtime and had driven up to Welcombe Mouth and trekked across the fields with their picnic to check out the iron age hill fort at Embury Beacon. Disappointingly, they were greeted by a sign that said seventy five percent of it had fallen into the sea. All that remained was a section of the eastern rampart. It was nothing to look at, just a ridge on a windy, weather beaten cliff.

"Should've checked first," her father had said, "Googled it. We could've just looked at the pictures and not bothered coming."

But Ella was glad they had come. Every minute was precious and the outdoors had a healing quality that she had never been able to explain. And she needed healing. They both needed that. Besides it was a clear day and she could see right the way across to Lundy and could even make out the Welsh hills across the Bristol Channel. Southwards was Tintagel Island and the wonderful stories of King Arthur. Like the Round Table knights, she had been searching for the Grail all her life, maybe this was the day she would find it. The thought made her feel expansive and stronger than she'd felt in a long time. Anything was possible.

"Look at me," she cried as she stood on the cliff edge and spread her arms, fluttering them gracefully in the strong breeze. She felt like she could take flight and soar through the air like a bird.

"Come away," shouted her father, "it's not safe so close to the edge."

"I bet if I jumped, I would fly like an eagle," she said

"For Christ sake, do as you're told," barked her father again, sounding angry and out of patience. A little voice inside her head told her this was her real father, not the loving, gentle one of her imagination. Besides, he had no right to be chastising her. She was eighteen and was not used to being told what to do, not since he had left, not by anyone.

But this was her father and the six year old girl he had left behind all those years ago, only wanted to please him. So she smiled and came away from the edge.

They set their picnic basket down in a deep gully, all that remained of the rampart, and laid out a blanket on the grass. They were sheltered from the strong wind here and could enjoy the warmth of the sun on their faces. It was a private place, a place where no one would disturb them.

The picnic hamper was soon emptied of its contents and Ella's father lay down on the blanket, complaining that he was tired after the morning's walk.

"Not as young as I used to be," he said, "Things change. I've changed."

With that he drifted away into an afternoon nap. She lay down beside him, head on his shoulder, gazing along his neck, speckled with stubble, rising to a strong jaw and wide mouth, gently turned up at the edges. Summer scents were mingling with the smell of his aftershave, deep and musky, like the smell of moist soil in spring rain. The music of the ocean filled her world and brought with it thoughts of forbidden fruit, of tender words and soft caresses, trapped like fluttering butterflies in a spider's web. Dreamily, she fell into its silky folds, floating down. Tumbling. Sinking. So soft. So warm. So safe.

As she dozed, an unexpected noise exploded in the distance, startling her into wakefulness. It was the sound of someone screaming, someone needing help. She shook her father but he was deep inside his own dreaming and did not stir. Jumping quickly to her feet, she left the shelter of the rampart and ran across a meadow that led down to a wood.

There she found a child, a young girl of no more than six years dressed in winter clothes, standing alone in the centre of a clearing, surrounded by a circle of holly trees.

She looked mournful and frightened.

"I can't move," she said, "something's holding me here."

"There's nothing here," Ella said, "Nothing but the wind blowing through the holly leaves." As she spoke she realised she could see through the girl as if looking through a smoky veil.

Without warning, the girl began to scream, "I'm trapped," she cried, "there's a terror here that you can't see. Please help me." She reached out her hand. "Closer, closer," she pleaded, "You must come closer. Take my hand, pull me free."

The child was so distraught that Ella had no choice. She reached out, their hands touched. Snap, the trap was sprung, the quarry captured. The child melted into the soft brown earth, leaving Ella alone, stranded, unable to move.

Her cries jolted her father from his slumber. In a moment he was on his feet, running and rolling down to where she stood, trapped in the middle of the holly grove.

"I can't move father," Ella cried, "I'm stuck."

"Hold on. I'll save you," he cried.

He began to chant a strange incantation. The sound echoed around the grove, haunting and chilling. They were words that spoke of pain, of fear, of dark deeds lost and forgotten in the mists of time. It was a banquet that beckoned the invisible terror, such a feast of fear in comparison to the meagre morsels offered by the child. It was a pluvial pit, full of confession and remorse. Ella felt the unseen tormentor leave her, felt it drawing away and taking the shadows with it. It seemed to fuse with her father, transforming him into a brown hare with wild eyes, whiskers twitching, sniffing the air, sniffing her scent. Mad March hare, looking for a mate, its eyes on her. She is old enough now to know that which it seeks is forbidden. She tries to draw away but she is held fast. The next moment, it is her father again, her protector, her saviour. His face contorts and changes as he struggles to keep hold of his reality. She knows he fights for his soul; he cannot succumb to this madness.

"Where are you father?"she cried, "The child is gone. What will become of me if you leave me again?"

His voice, broken and fragmented like a clay pot thrown against a wall, comes out of the mouth of the hare,

"You are mine, you belong to me."

"Father! Where are you?"

"I am here," he cried, the fatherly face fading back, words strangled between two worlds.

"Leave me Ella. Run for your life."

"I cannot father. I am bound to you."

A voice inside her head – 'run, Ella, run'.

"Come my child, let me burrow again into your depths, hollow you out and swim in your river. Flesh against fur. Warm. Comforting. Gentle."

'Run Ella. Run.'

A loud noise; the crackle of a lightning strike. The earth shuddered.

A frog is sitting on the heavy branch of a fallen oak. It is the fattest, greenest frog Ella has ever seen.

He smiled as he croaked,

"I was once a tadpole, and look at me now. The finest figure of a frog you ever saw. I could be your Prince, little Princess, if you will help me."

"I don't want to help you," she cried, "I must help my father. He fights for his soul."

"You cannot help your father. Your father lost his soul a long time ago. Do you not remember?"

Ella wept because she could not remember.

"I can save you, little Princess. Pick me up and stroke my cool back. In my eyes you will see a world of transformation, where all can be healed. Come, little Princess, come and find the story that will set you free."

Ella stooped down and the frog leapt into her hand. In that moment she remembered things she did not even know she had forgotten, the warmth of a mother's touch, the sweet scent of pine, a house far away where bread was baked in the kitchen and clothes hung to dry in the scullery, a yellow dress billowing on a windy day, running through fields, red shoes pinching toes. A place where God lived in the clouds and always answered the prayers sent to Him. All except one. The most important one. A father walking away. A mother weeping for the lost innocence of a daughter, and then weeping again because her warm home was to be swapped for a cold grave. A father who returned too late.

"Cast me up to the clouds, little Princess and I will take you with me," said the frog.

Ella raised her arm and threw him high into the air, as hard as she could. He twirled around and around, his wet body glinting in the sunlight. As he flew he began to sing, she had never heard such a beautiful song. He sang with the harmony of the ocean and the joy of a thousand angels. He grew wings and became an eagle, soaring higher and higher into the summer sky until he was nothing more than a tiny black speck, smaller than a gnat and yet larger than the whole Universe.

The man was mesmerised.

The hare was hypnotised.

Only the child was free.

Ella fell to the ground, sinking deep into the embrace of the warm earth. The love that was surrounding her was healing her, lifting her up. Home at last.

She sighed gently as a dragonfly alighted on her soft pink lips, its damask wings reflecting the rainbows of the sun. The fat, green frog, seeing his chance, leapt onto her chest. One flick of its sticky tongue and the dragonfly was gone from the world.

Ella's father gathered his daughter up into his arms. Now it was his turn to weep. The burden he carried was far more than the weight of his daughter's body.

As he made his way back to the car, wild hares danced round each other in their mating ritual, hitting each other with soft paws, like friends in a playground brawl.

*'Picnic At Embury Beacon'*

Embury Beacon is the site of an Iron Age promontory fort on the west of the Hartland Peninsula in North Devon. The fort has been almost entirely lost to coastal erosion, but some of the Eastern Ramparts still remain on the cliff top.

On my trek along the South West Coast Path, I stopped here to eat my lunch and, whilst admiring the inland views, I was reminded of a dream I had long ago - a dream that eventually gave rise to this story.

If you've enjoyed this collection of short stories,

look out for more

# Twisted Tales

## written on the South West Coast Path

**Twisted Tales of Cornwall**

**Twisted Tales of South Devon**

**Twisted Tales of Dorset**

As a self-published writer, the author needs and encourages reviews on Amazon and/or Goodreads. If you prefer, you can email your feedback via her website www.docdreamuk.com

## About the Author

Jo is divorced with two grown up sons. She suffers from CWD, (Compulsive Writing Disorder), and has been scribbling down stories since she was knee high to a grasshopper. After too many careers, she decided to fulfil a lifelong ambition and go to University to study Science. On gaining a PhD in Chemistry, she secured a teaching position at the University of Nottingham and moved to a sleepy village in the East Midlands where she lived and worked in academia for over fifteen years. In 2011, after much soul searching, she finally departed the stage of 'normal' work in order to devote her life to writing.

Born and bred in Saddleworth, in the West Riding of Yorkshire, it wasn't long before the rugged Pennine landscape was calling her back home. She now lives in the village of Greenfield on the edge of the Dark Peak.

***Leaving Ilfracombe.***

Printed in Great Britain
by Amazon

45469515R10050